Padma Shri Pran

Maurice Horn, the editor of World Encyclopedia of Comics, has described cartoonist PRAN as Walt Disney of India.

Entertaining generation after generation, his comics have been constant companion of all the growing youngsters providing fun and amusement through his famous characters like CHACHA CHAUDHARY, SABU, SHRIMATIJI, PINKI, BILLOO, RAMAN etc. More than 600 of his titles are selling well in the market, and numerous comic strips are regularly appearing in various newspapers. His CHACHA CHAUDHARY comics had already been adapted for a TV Serial, and ran continuously for 600 episodes on a premier channel.

Travelling widely over the globe, he delivers lectures at various International Conferences. He has also been honoured with 'People of The Year Award' by Limca Book of Records for popularizing comics. His comic book 'United We Stand' was released in 1983 by the then Prime Minister Mrs. Indira Gandhi, and is still very popular among children.

Publisher

SOMEONE MUST BE ILL.

I'LL CHECK.

YOUR GRANDMA IS OLD. HER TEETH MUST BE INFECTED. I'LL CHECK.

OPEN YOUR MOUTH NANI.

NO NEED TO OPEN MOUTH FOR SHOWING TEETH.

YOU CAN SEE THEM LIKE THIS.
!!

YOUR DADAJI MUST BE UNWELL.

I'LL CHECK HIM...

OUCH!
BANG!!

OH!
THUD!

DR. BAGWANE.
ARE YOU OK?
OH... YES...

YES! I'M FINE.

I'LL SURELY FIND A PATIENT IN YOUR HOME. THIS SQUIRREL.
NOTHING HAPPENS TO KUTKUT.

NEVER SAY THAT.

MAYBE SHE IS UNWELL.

I'LL CHECK HER.

CHEEE !!

OUCH !
AAHH !

WHAMM !

OWWW !

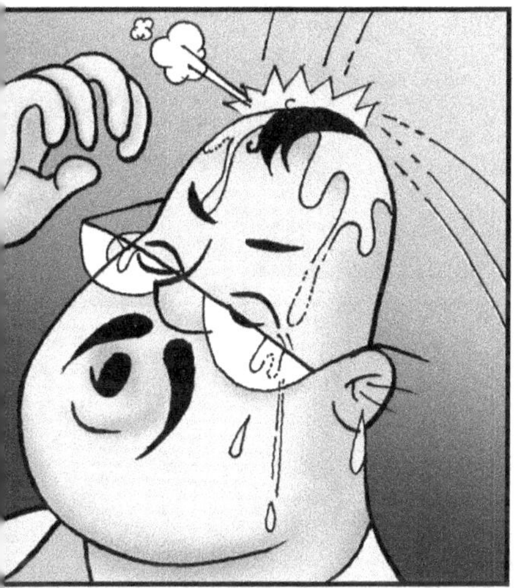

WHERE AM I?

CONGRATS
OR BAGWANE.
YOU FOUND A PATIENT IN OUR HOUSE.

AND THAT'S YOU.

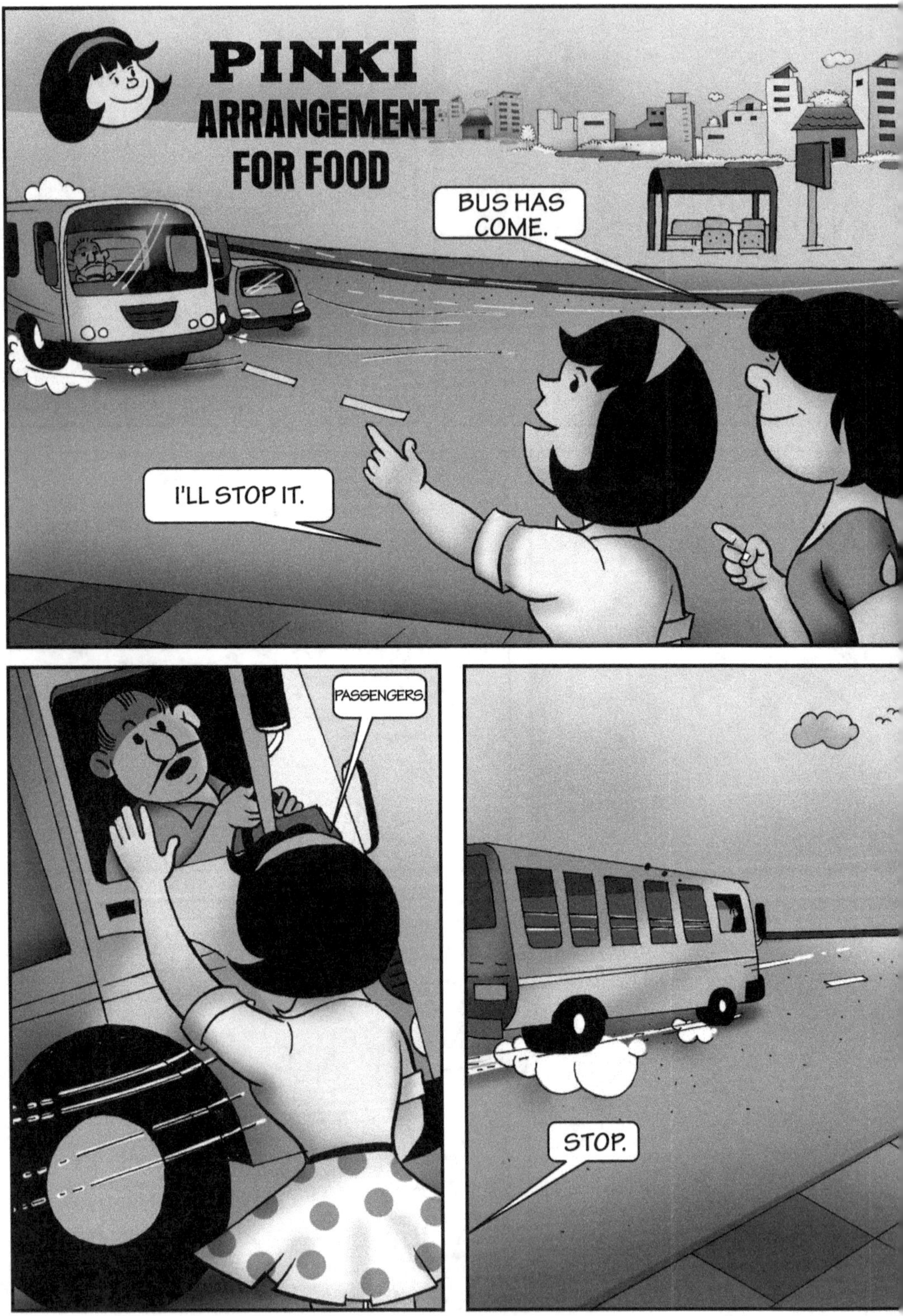

PINKI
ARRANGEMENT FOR FOOD

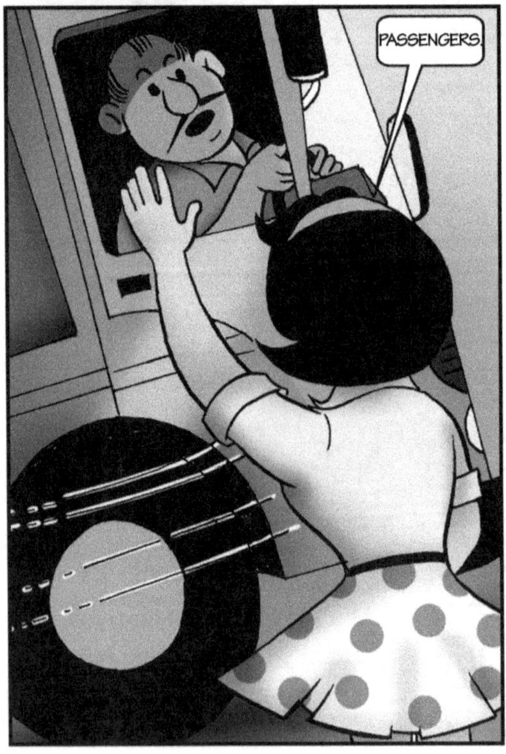

SCREECH !!

WHERE DO YOU WANT TO GO ?
DON'T HAVE TO GO. WE HAD A BET THAT THE CONDUCTOR OF THE NEXT BUS WILL HAVE MOUSTACHES.

SO I STOPPED THE BUS.

I LOST THE BET. YOU DON'T HAVE MOUSTACHES.

I'M STARTING TO FEEL HUNGRY PINKI !
SEE, SHUHINA AUNTY LIVES THERE. LET'S GO AND HAVE SOMETHING THERE.

NOT AT ALL. YOU DON'T KNOW HER. SHE GETS ANGRY FOR PETTY REASONS.

IN HER ANGER SHE PICKS UP ANYTHING AND HITS OTHERS.
OH !!

AUNTY HAS LOTS OF FRUITS.

IN THAT CASE OUR FOOD HAS BEEN ARRANGED.

HI ! PINKI.
HI ! SHUHINA AUNTY.
© PRAN'S FEATURE

8

AUNTY, I'M REMINDED OF A NICE THING ON SEEING YOUR NOSE.
OK! WHAT'S THAT?

PAKODA.

GRRR! PINKI HOW DARE YOU??
MY NOSE LIKE PAKODA??

GRRR!!
GRRR!!
GRRR!!

CATCH IT.

GRRR !!

THAT'S IT AUNTY.

OUR FOOD HAS BEEN ARRANGED.

PRAN
CHACHA CHAUDHARY
AND
CRISPY'S MAGIC

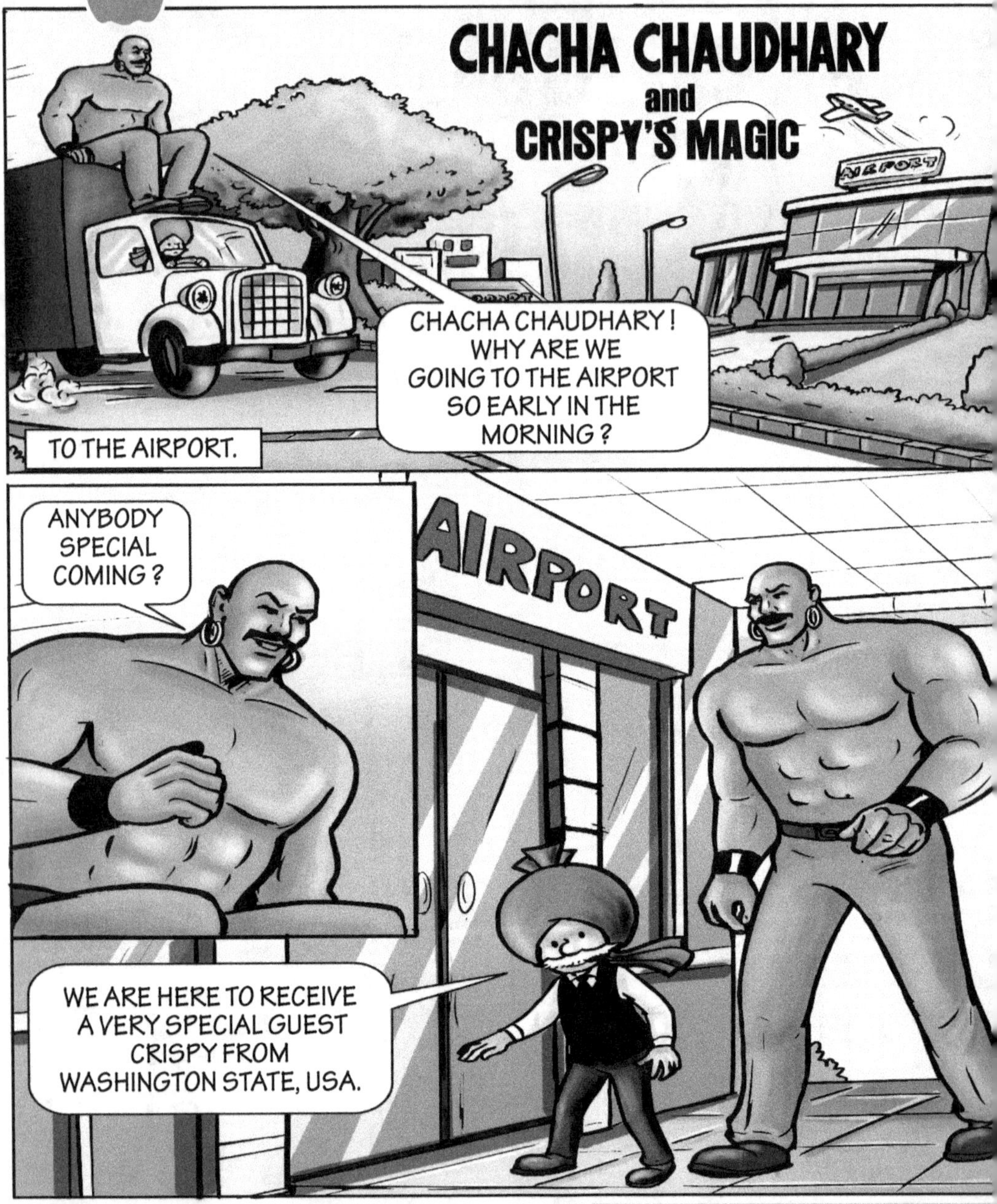

CHACHA CHAUDHARY
and
CRISPY'S MAGIC

WASHINGTON

I'VE NEVER HEARD THIS NAME BEFORE.

WASHINGTON STATE PRODUCES THE BEST APPLES IN THE WORLD.

LOCATED IN THE PACIFIC NORTH WEST OF AMERICA, WASHINGTON APPLES HAVE MORE THAN 1,70,000 ACRE AREA WHERE THESE ARE GROWN.

HERE THE BEST APPLES OF DIFFERENT VARIETIES, TASTE, FLAVOUR AND COLOR ARE GROWN.

YOUR SECRET TO SHARP BRAIN IS AN APPLE A DAY.

3000 FT ABOVE THE SEA LEVEL, THEY ARE CULTIVATED WITH FRESH WATER RICH IN MINERALS.

Tasty delight

WASHINGTON
No other apple comes close.
apples@scs-group.com • bestapples.com
facebook.com/WashingtonApples.India
twitter.com/WApplesIndia

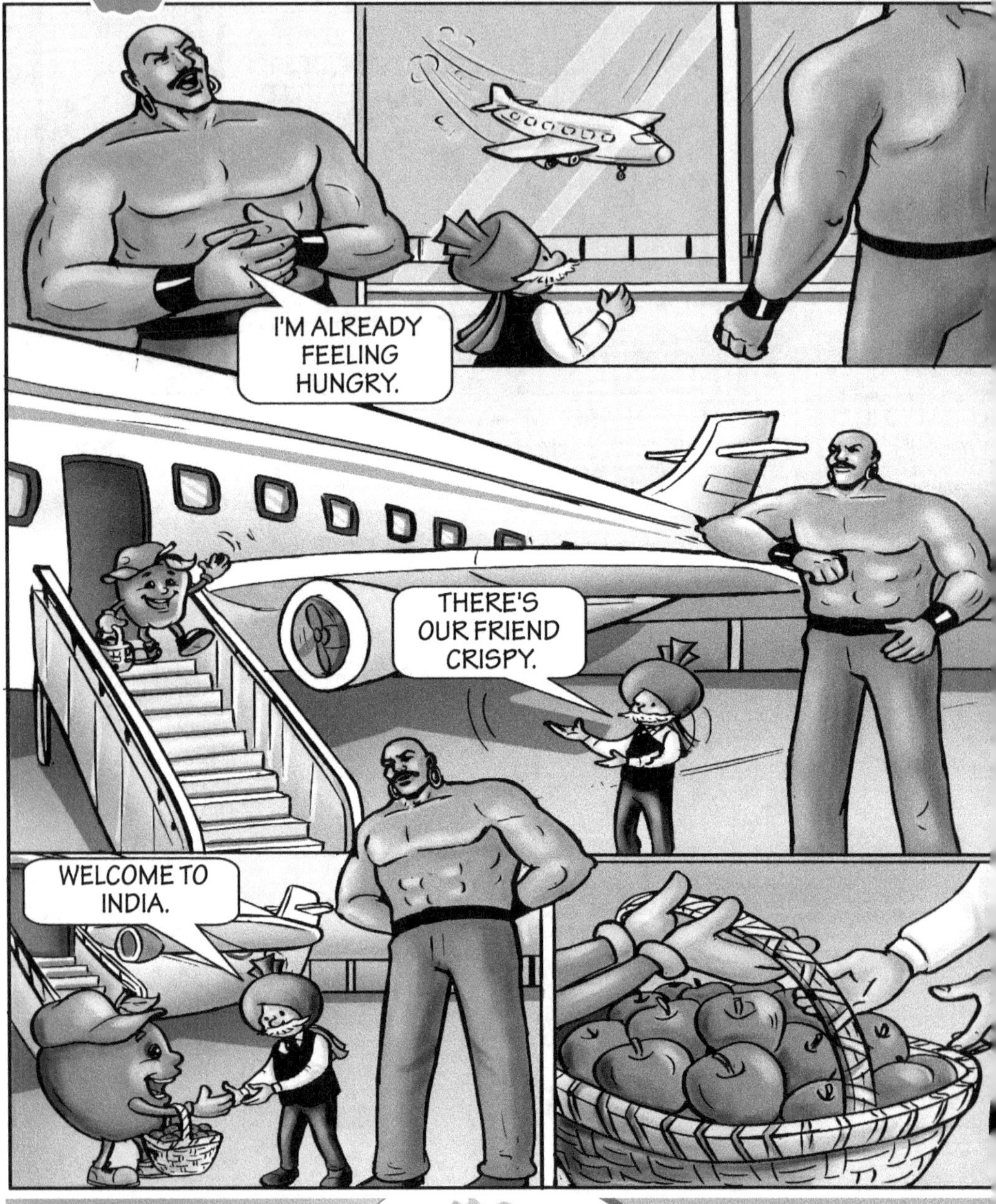

WASHINGTON

I'M ALREADY FEELING HUNGRY.
THERE'S OUR FRIEND CRISPY.
WELCOME TO INDIA.

Wholesome health

WASHINGTON
No other apple comes close.
apples@scs-group.com • bestapples.com
facebook.com/WashingtonApples.India
twitter.com/WApplesIndia

WASHINGTON

MY INTELLIGENCE SOURCES HAVE TOLD THAT CRISPY FROM AMERICA HAS COME TO INDIA.
IF WE KIDNAP HIM, WE CAN DEMAND A GOOD RANSOM.
HALT ! WE ARE GOING TO KIDNAP CRISPY.
WE'VE HEARD THAT YOU HAVE BROUGHT APPLES FROM WASHINGTON STATE.
THEY ARE AT BACK OF DUGDUG.

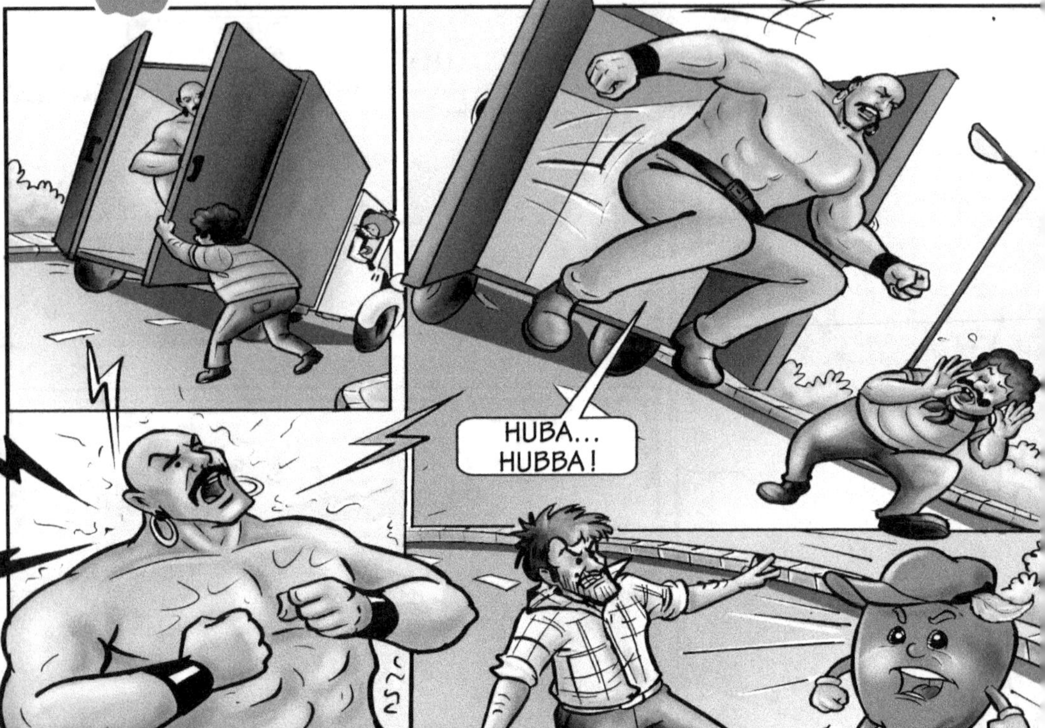

HUBA...
HUBBA !

THUD D !

SWOOSH !

A medium Washington Apple contains about five grams of fiber, more than most cereals.

Washington
Apples
Wholesome health
Healthy eating doesn't get better than this.
Every bite of Washington apples is filled
with juicy goodness.
So go ahead, take another bite!
apples@scs-group.com • bestapples.com
facebook.com/WashingtonApples.India
twitter.com/WApplesIndia
WASHINGTON
No other appl
comes close.

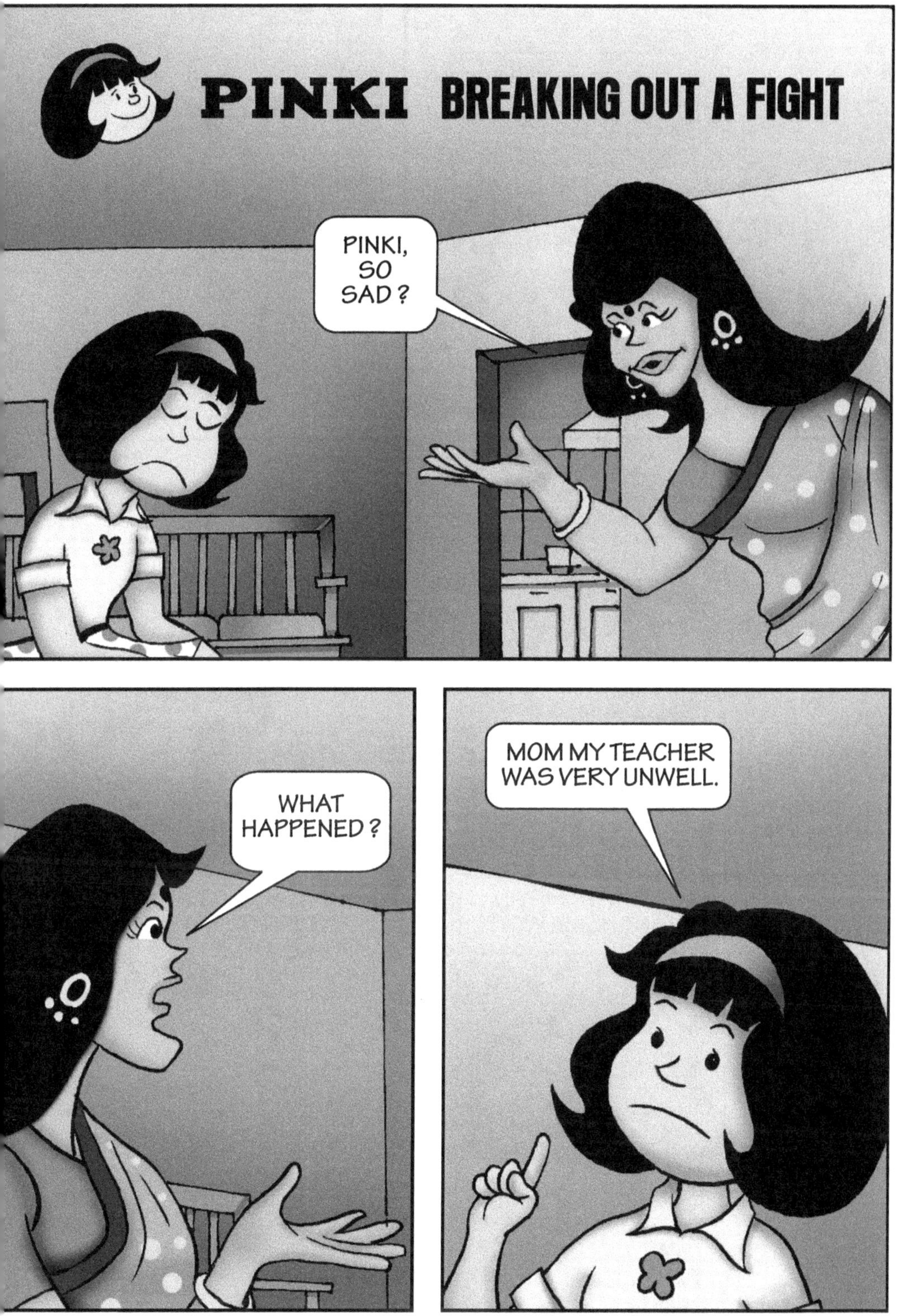

PINKI BREAKING OUT A FIGHT

SO ? IS SHE MORE ILL NOW ?

NO.

SHE'S PERFECTLY FINE NOW.

SHE'D GIVEN ME AN IMPORTANT HOME WORK.

BUT I HAVEN'T BEEN ABLE TO FINISH IT AS YET.

DON'T BE SAD PINKI

TELL ME THE TOPIC, I'LL HELP YOU.

THE TOPIC IS... HOW DOES A FIGHT BREAK OUT ?

IS IT A DIFFICULT TOPIC PAPA ?

NOT AT ALL. I'LL EXPLAIN.

IMAGINE THAT YOUR MOM AND HER FRIEND ARGUE ON A NEW SAREE.

WAIT A MINUTE. GIVING SUCH NEGATIVE EXAMPLES TO A CHILD ?

IT'S MISLEADING THE CHILD.

SEE I'M NOT MISLEADING HER.

YES YOU'RE DOING SO.

YOU BE QUIET.

YOU BE QUIET.
YOU...
BOTH OF YOU BE QUIET.

I'VE UNDERSTOOD HOW A FIGHT BREAKS OUT.

23

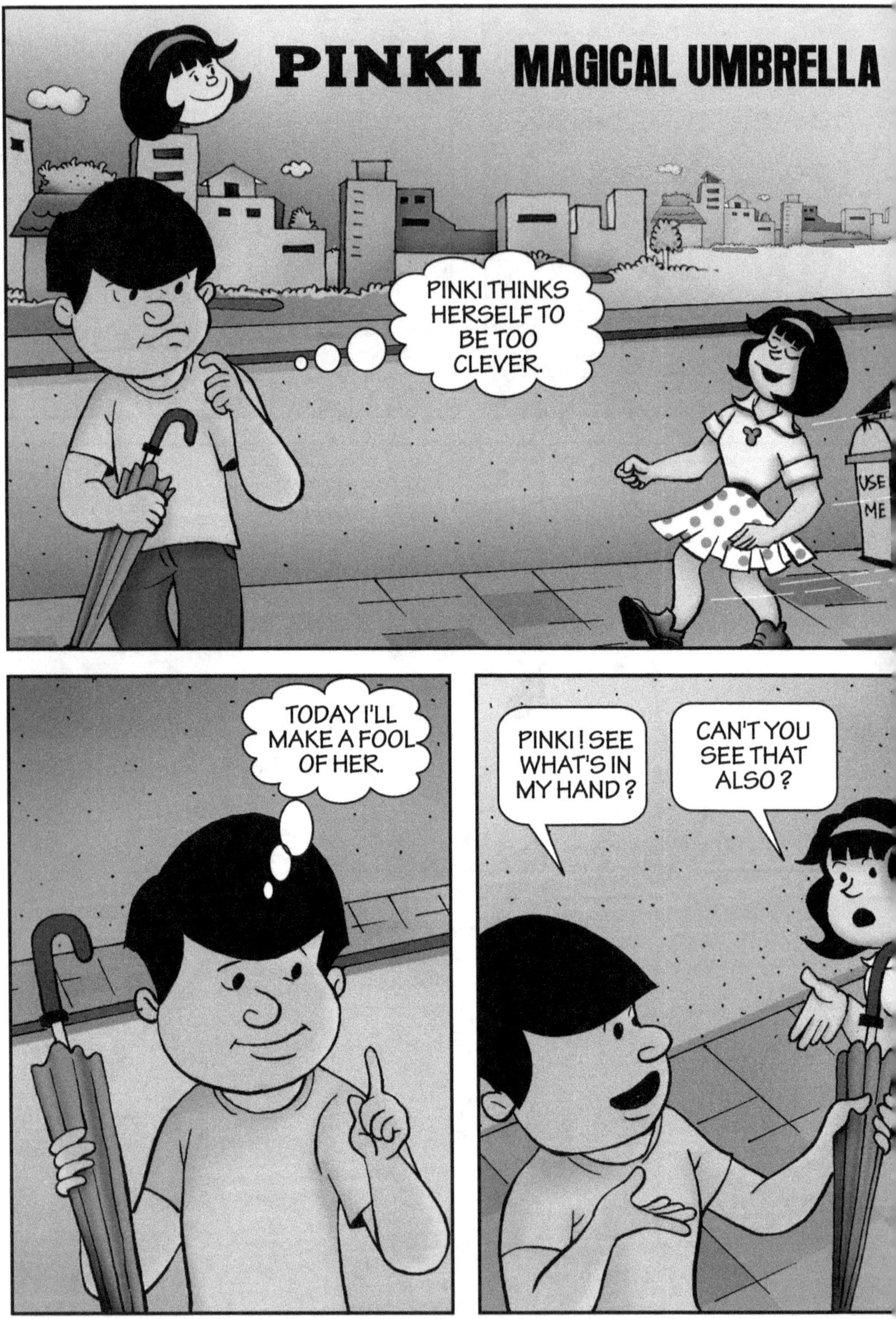

PINKI MAGICAL UMBRELLA

THIS IS A MAGIC UMBRELLA.
RED COLOURED UMBRELLA.

WHOSOEVER COMES UNDER THIS WILL THINK OF YOU ONLY.

TAKE IT AND RETURN IN THE EVENING.
OK.

UMBRELLA TO SAVE FROM SUN.

CAN I COME UNDER YOUR UMBRELLA?
WHY NOT, NIKKI?

A FEW DAYS BACK I BORROWED MONEY FROM YOU.

HERE IS IT.

WHY ARE YOU WALKING IN THE SUN? COME HERE.

THANKS PINKI.

HERE YOU ALSO HAVE A CHOCOLATE.

WOW! RONNIE IS SHARING HIS CHOCOLATE.

IT SURELY IS A MAGIC UMBRELLA.

RAPATJI, IF YOU WANT PROTECTION FROM THE SUN THEN COME HERE.

THANKS, PINKI.

I'VE BOUGHT A NEW GAME. WHENEVER YOU WANT TO PLAY IT, COME TO MY HOUSE.

THIS UMBRELLA HAS DONE WONDERS.

IN THE EVENING...
THIS UMBRELLA IS REALLY MAGICAL.

IT ACTUALLY DID WONDERS.

I WANTED TO FOOL PINKI. FORTUNATELY SOMETHING GOOD HAPPENED TO HER.

THAT TOO BECAUSE OF MY UMBRELLA.

CAN SOMEONE ACTUALLY FOLLOW A PERSON BECAUSE OF AN UMBRELLA ?
GRRR !!

GRRR !!
HELP !

BULL'S AFTER YOU... SURELY YOUR UMBRELLA IS MAGICAL.
© PRAN'S FEATURES

PINKI SERIOUS AILMENT
WHY ARE YOU SO TROUBLED BHOLU PEHALWAN ?
I DON'T KNOW WHY SUDDENLY MY LEGS ARE TURNING BLUE.

OH ! A BODY PART TURNS BLUE ONLY WHEN POISON SPREADS THERE.

APPEARS TO BE A SERIOUS DISEASE.

I'LL JUST GET ITS REMEDY.

NOW MY GRANDFATHER'S BOOK OF TRADITIONAL REMEDIES WILL BE HELPFUL.

THIS HAS THE REMEDY TO YOUR LEGS TURNING BLUE.

IT'S A BIT EXPENSIVE.
NEVER MIND.

SOON...
IT COST RS. 10,000.
SO WHAT ?

IT WILL CURE THE
AILMENT OF YOUR LEGS.

AFTER SOME DAYS..
SOB !!
WHAT HAPPENED?

MY LEGS
ARE STILL
BLUE.
OH! IT SEEMS
TO BE SERIOUS
THAN WE
THOUGHT.

IT TELLS ABOUT AN OIL
FOR SUCH A DISEASE.
IT'S COSTLY, BUT VERY
EFFECTIVE.

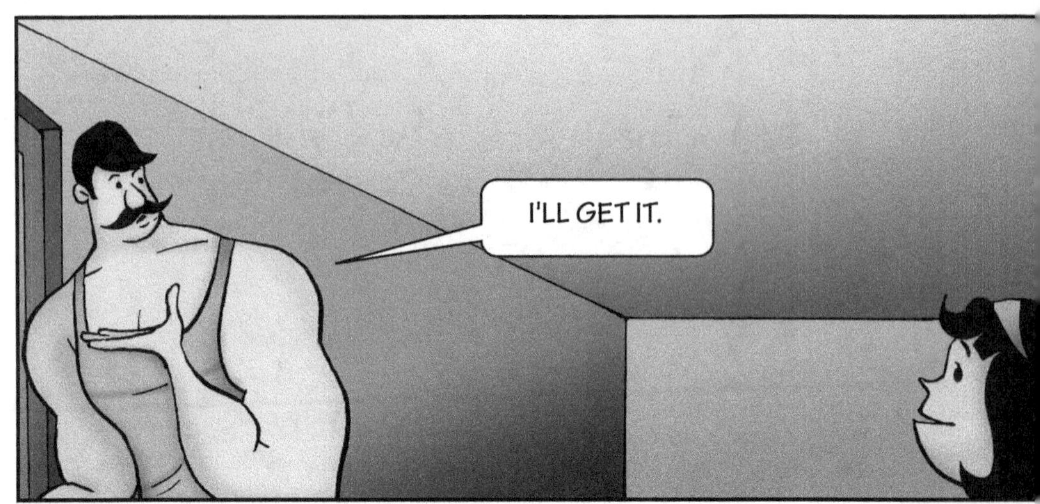

I'LL GET IT.

GOOD! NOW APPLY THIS OIL ON YOUR LEGS.

YOU'LL BE FINE.

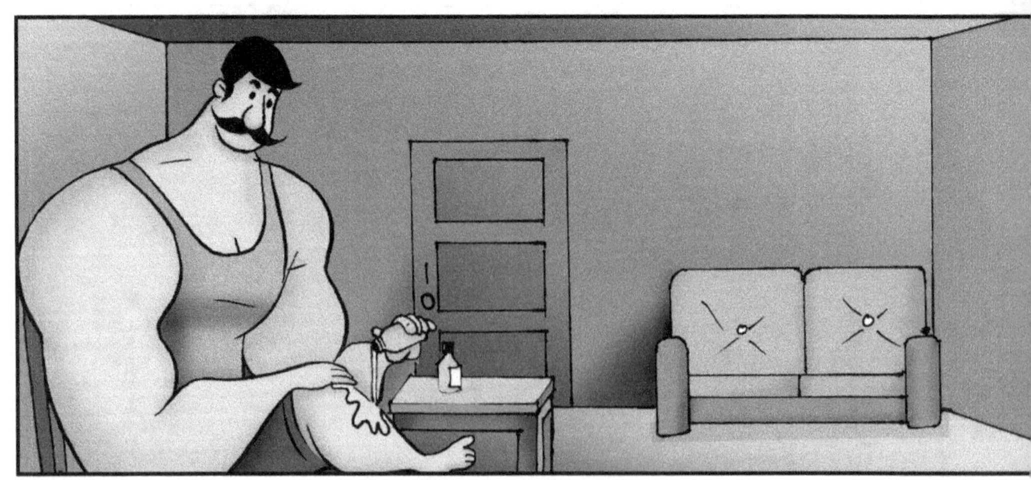

SOB !!
NOW WHAT HAPPENED BHOLU PEHALWAN ?

SEE !

THE COLOUR OF YOUR LEGS REVEALS ONLY ONE THING...

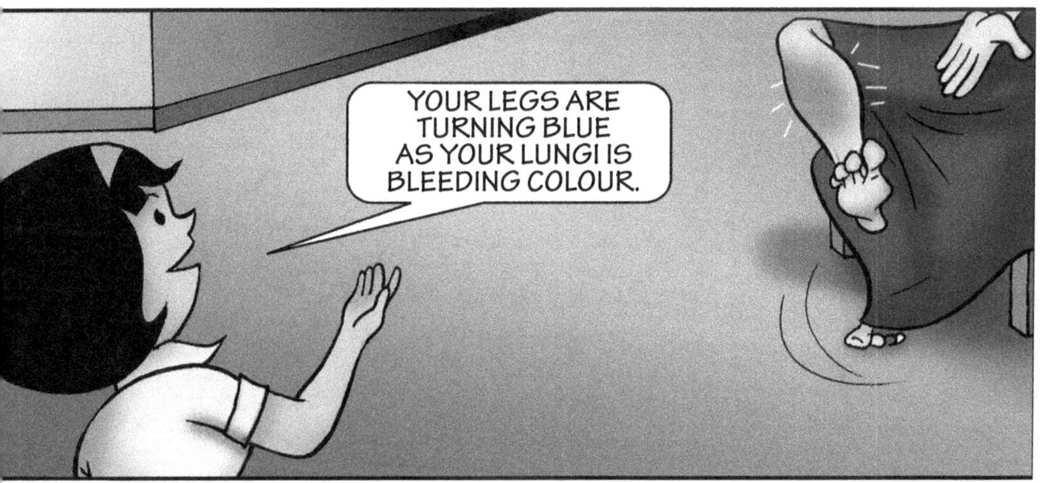

YOUR LEGS ARE TURNING BLUE AS YOUR LUNGI IS BLEEDING COLOUR.

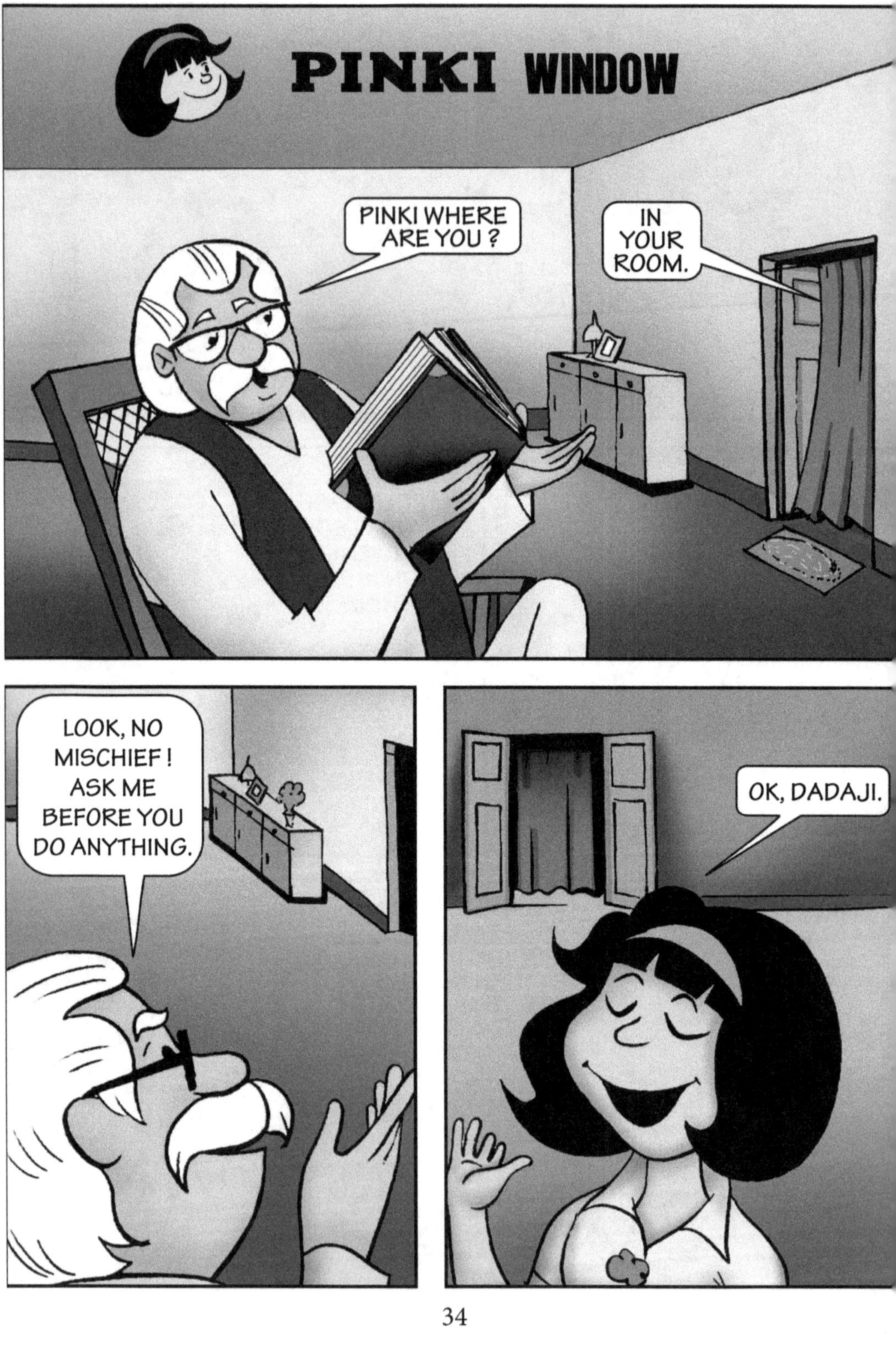

PINKI WINDOW

SOON...
IT SEEMS I'LL HAVE TO ASK HIM.

DADAJI !
PINKI I AM DOING SOMETHING VERY IMPORTANT. DON'T DISTURB ME.

DADAJI THAT...
OK BE QUICK AND TELL.

DADAJI I AM UNABLE TO OPEN THE WINDOW.

THAT'S IT ?? POUR SOME HOT OIL, IT WILL OPEN.

DADAJI BUT...
LOOK HERE PINKI. DON'T WASTE TIME BY ASKING SO MANY QUESTIONS.

GO AND DO AS I SAID.

OK.

SOON...
DADAJI!
PINKI, YOU?

OK, NOW WHAT?
DADAJI, STILL THE WINDOW ISN'T OPENING.

EVEN AFTER POURING OIL?
NO.

THEN DO ONE THING. HIT IT SOFTLY. IT'LL OPEN.
BUT DADAJI?

PINKI!
SORRY DADAJI, I'LL GO AND DO AS YOU SAID.

GOOD GIRL.

SOON...
SMASH!
OH!

WHAT DID PINKI BREAK?

OH GOD! MY LAPTOP!

WHY DID YOU BREAK THE LAPTOP PINKI?
I WAS TRYING TO OPEN ITS WINDOW. YOU ONLY TOLD ME TO POUR OIL IN IT.

THEN YOU TOLD TO HIT IT AND THIS IS THE RESULT.

OH GOD! HOW COULD I KNOW YOU WERE TALKING OF COMPUTER WINDOW?

PINKI
BABA KALANDAR

LISTEN… LISTEN!
ALL YOUR WISHES
WILL BE FULFILLED
BY KALANDAR
MAHARAJ.
HOT
SOAP

BABA! TODAY'S
MY CRICKET
MATCH.
CHILD, YOU'LL HIT A
CENTURY BY EATING
BABA'S PRASAD.
PRICE RS. 51.

I WANT IT.
HERE'S THE
MONEY.

GOLDEN CHANCE!
TAKE PRASAD
AND SUCCESS IS
YOURS.
PINKI!
I ALSO WANT
PRASAD.
CHAMPU!
COME
WITH
ME.

CHILD, TAKE THIS. VICTORY
WILL BE YOURS.

SWOOSH !!

THUDD !!

OUTTT !
HOW COULD THIS HAPPEN? BABA KALANDAR SAID I'LL HIT A CENTURY. I'VE TAKEN HIS PRASAD.

AND I'VE TAKEN DOUBLE PRASAD BY PAYING HIM RS. 101. HE BLESSED ME THAT I WILL KNOCK OUT THE BATSMAN WITH MY BALL
ऐसा ?

RUN !!

PINKI
POP SINGER

HERE'S A TICKET FOR FOREIGN TOUR. GO ABROAD AND BE A SENSATION.
THANKS. YOU'RE A TRUE BENEFACTOR.

MY AC CAR'S READY TO DROP YOU AT THE AIRPORT.

BYE !! MICHAEL JACKSON JUNIOR !
YOU WON'T BE ABLE TO DISTURB ANYONE THERE.
SIR! WHERE HAVE YOU SENT HIM ?

WHERE THAT HOARSE SINGER CAN'T DISTURB ANYONE.
IS THERE SUCH A PLACE ?

SAHARA DESERT ! NOBODY CAN BE TRAUMATIZED BY HIS CACOPHONY THERE.

PINKI
BADMINTON

GO OUT AND PLAY.
DON'T INCREASE THE
ELECTRICITY BILL BY
WATCHING SO MUCH
TV.

SILKY ! YOU'RE
ALWAYS EATING.
YOU SHOULD TAKE
EXERCISE.

EATING IS EXERCISE
FOR THE TEETH.

LET'S PLAY
BADMINTON.
OK. IF
YOU SAY
SO.
CLUB

TAPPPP !!

HERE IS MY SHOT !
SWISHHH !!

NAUGHTY GIRLS ! YOU'VE TORN THE CLUB'S NET.

RUN SILKY !!

MRS. MADHU HERE'S A BILL RS. 5000. YOU & SILKY'S MO WILL SHARE IT.
BILL ??
YES ! PINKY AND SILKY HAVE TORN THE CLUB'S NET.

PINKI
DRAMA

BRITISH !
WE AREN'T
WEAKLINGS.
EVERY CHILD CAN
SACRIFICE HIS
LIFE FOR HIS
MOTHER
LAND.

WE NEVER CAME
TO OCCUPY YOUR
COUNTRY, SO
WHY HAVE YOU
COME TO USURP
OUR LAND ?

REMEMBER ! YOU
CAN'T STAY HERE.
YOU'LL HAVE TO
LEAVE FROM HERE.
PINKI'S TALKING TO
A POLE. HAS SHE
GONE WACKY ?

LET ME CLICK A PROOF
OF PINKI'S WEIRDNESS.
I'LL SHARE IT WITH MY
FRIENDS. ALL WILL
MAKE FUN
OF
HER.

YOU ARE
SCARING US
WITH A
WAR...
WE'RE NOT
AFRAID.
I'LL GO CLOSER
AND CLICK.

GO BACK BRITISHERS !

THEN.
STRIKE !

THUDDD !!!

PINKI, YOUR STICK SAVED MY CAMERA. OTHERWISE THE BALL WOULD'VE HIT MY CAMERA.
GARO, YOU ?

I SAW YOU TALKING TO THE POLE AND THOUGHT YOU'VE GOING CRAZY.
I WAS REHEARSING FOR THE DRAMA.

www.chachachaudhary.com

CONSTABLE GATKA ! I SAW ONE THIEF.
WHERE ?

HE WAS HERE A LITTLE WHILE AGO.
TRYING TO FOOL ME ?
कॉर्पोरेशन कुडेदान

SNEEZE !
SNEEZING SOUND. THAT THIEF HAD COLD.

YES ! HE'S THERE.
COME DOWN.

THANKS PINKI ! NOW I'LL GET A PROMOTION.

www.ingramcontent.com/pod-product-compliance
Lightning Source LLC
Chambersburg PA
CBHW050619160726
48003CB00003B/1254